sky
rat

that
pesky
rat

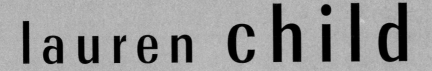

lauren child

TED SMART

Thank you
Randala
and Albena

Look out for Lauren Child's
Clarice Bean books
and the award-winning
I will not ever
NEVER
eat a tomato

and for anyone who
has ever wished the
were somebody's p

Max

Louie

Lucy

Zaida

Sam

and for fabulous
Frances and her
pets Lucy, Sam,
Ata and Cui

This book is for
the gorgeous Max
and her little
dog Louie

Flame

Sita

Twinkle

Ata & Cui

with love to Jo and Thomas,
long-suffering owners of Twinkle,
the Bette Davis of cats

Cheeky

Donut

Orchard Books, 96 Leonard Street,
London EC2A 4XD
Orchard Books Australia
32/45-51 Huntley Street,
Alexandria, NSW 2015
This edition produced for
The Book People Ltd
Hall Wood Avenue, Haydock,
St Helens WA11 9UL
First published in
Great Britain in 2002
ISBN 1 84362 369 2
Copyright © Lauren Child 2002

This is me.
I'm the one with the **pointy** nose and b e a d y eyes.
The cutesy one in the middle.

I live in dustbin number **3**, **Grubby** Alley.

Every now and again I come back to find someone has emptied all my belongings into a **big** van and driven off with them.
It's very **upsetting**.

I'm a brown rat, a street rat.
But people call me that pesky rat.
I don't know why.
They say I smell,
but that's not my fault, it's the dirt.

Sometimes when I am tucked into
my crisp packet,
I look up at all the cosy windows
and wonder what it would be like
to live with creature comforts.
To belong to somebody.
To be an actual pet.

Most of all I would like

to have a **name**, instead of just that **pesky rat**.

My friend Pierre,

who is a **chinchilla**,

is looked after by a rich lady called Madame Fifi.

He has a very **glamorous** life.

He lives in the lap of **luxury**.

Then there's this **Siamese** cat called **Oscar**. He lives with **Mr Washington**, a **busy** businessman.

Mr Washington is **always** at work so he doesn't have time to **wash fur** or be **strict**.

I'm quite good in the kitchen

but I hate

to be

bored.

Nibbles says, "It is fun hopping through hoops in a tutu. But sometimes I could do with taking off the clown's nose and putting my feet up."

You were divine darling!

Maybe it's all a bit n**e**r**v**e **wracking** for me.

I think I'd quite like one of those owners
who do lots of **sitting about**
like **Miss StClair.**

Her **Scottie** dog, Andrew, is always sitting by the

fire, having supper on a tray and they spend the evenings doing

Puzzles

together.

Andrew says,

"On the whole I feel

very well

looked after.

And

Miss StClair

is good company.

But it's rather

embarrassing

when we go out shopping."

Miss

StClair

makes

Andrew wear a little hat and coat.

So in the morning
I go to the pet shop
and ask Mrs Trill

if she has

an **owner**

who might **want** me.

She says,

"There isn't much call for brown rats, 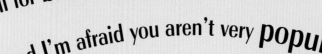 and I'm afraid you aren't very **popular** with the public."

I say,

"I don't see why **not**. I'm very good **company**, always **popping** up when you least expect me to, and I am happy to eat **anything**, even if it's been slightly **nibbled**."

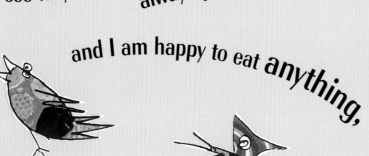

Mrs Trill says,

"Well, you could always make a **notice** and put it in the **window**. **You never know**."

So I write:

Me

Brown cat looking for kindly owner
with an interest in cheese
Hobbies include nibbling and chewing
would like a collar with my name on
would like a name
would prefer no baths
will wear a jumper if pushed
Yours keenly
            Brown rat (that pesky rat)
P.S sorry about bad paw writing

not
a very good picture

Then I wait **and** I wait

and I wait. Until . . .

. . . on Tuesday old Mr Fortesque is passing
and he **stops** to look at my **notice.**

He has to really **squint** because he
has such **bad** eyesight.

Then he looks at me and says,

"**My,**
haven't you
got a pointy nose
and, goodness me,
what a long tail, and such

unusual beady eyes . . .

I'll take him."

I can't
believe my **luck,**
nor can Mrs Trill.

Mrs Trill says,
"Are you **sure?**"

And **Mr Fortesque says,**
"Oh yes, I've been looking for a **brown cat**
as **nice** as this one for **ages.**"

Mrs Trill looks at **me** and **I** look at **Mrs Trill,**
and we **both** look at my notice,

but neither of us
says a word.

I just **love** being a **pet.**
And . . . I am trying to be **really** helpful.

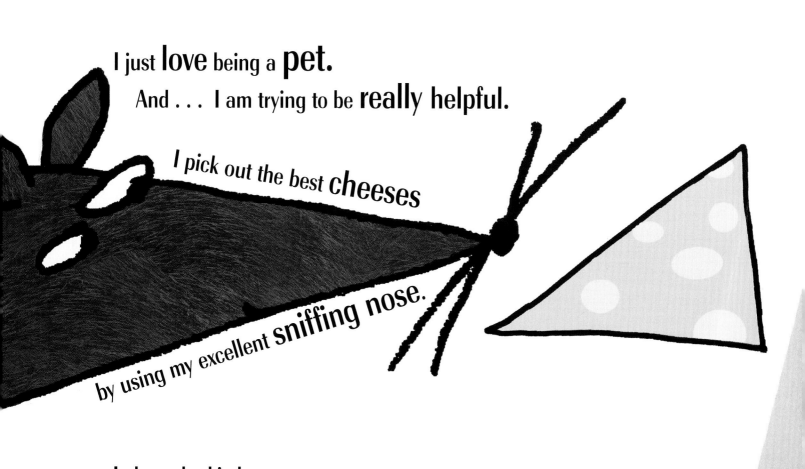

I pick out the best **cheeses**
by using my excellent sniffing nose.

I clean the kitchen
by n i b b l i n g
up the
c r u m b s.

I help Mr Fortesque

I cross the road by **scaring** the traffic.

And I'm **always** there when he comes **home**.

So here I am.

Finally a **pet** with a **name.**

So what
if I have to
wear a little
jumper?

Mr Fortesque says, "Well, Tiddles, who's a pretty **kittycat?**"

And I squeak, **"I am!"**

that
pes